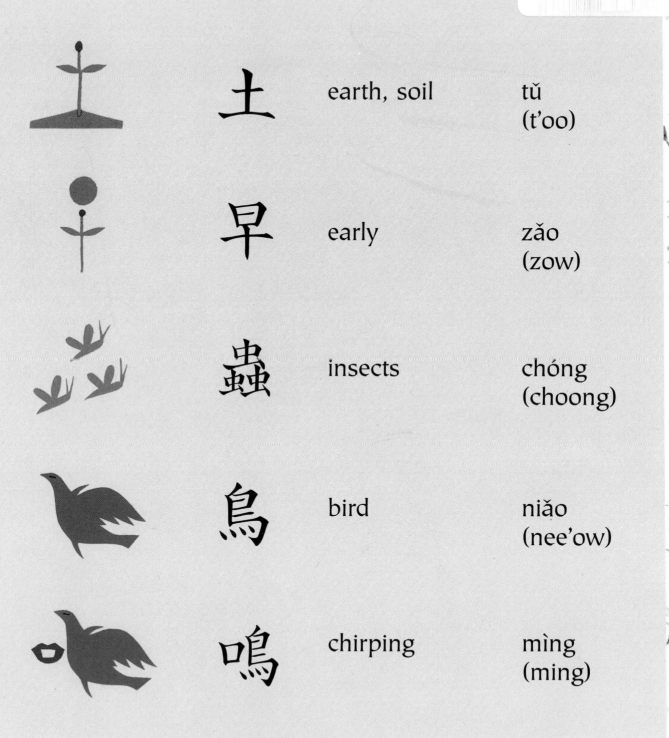

土 earth, soil tǔ (t'oo)

早 early zǎo (zow)

蟲 insects chóng (choong)

鳥 bird niǎo (nee'ow)

鳴 chirping mìng (ming)

Pronunciation of words in parentheses are
approximations of Mandarin Chinese.

Henry Holt and Company, Inc., *Publishers since 1866*
115 West 18th Street, New York, New York 10011
Henry Holt is a registered trademark of
Henry Holt and Company, Inc.

Published in Canada by Fitzhenry & Whiteside Ltd.,
195 Allstate Parkway, Markham, Ontario L3R 4T8.

Library of Congress Cataloging-in-Publication Data
Lee, Huy Voun. In the park / Huy Voun Lee.
Summary: On the first day of spring, a mother and her son go to
the park where they draw Chinese characters that represent words
relating to the season.
[1. Chinese language—Fiction. 2. Spring—Fiction.
3. Mother and sons—Fiction. 4. Chinese Americans—Fiction.]
I. Title. PZ7.L512481I 1997 [E]—dc21 97-24430

ISBN 0-8050-4128-1 First Edition—1998
10 9 8 7 6 5 4 3 2 1
Printed in the United States of America on acid-free paper.∞
The artist used cut-paper collage to create the illustrations for this book.

For Laura
— H.V.L.

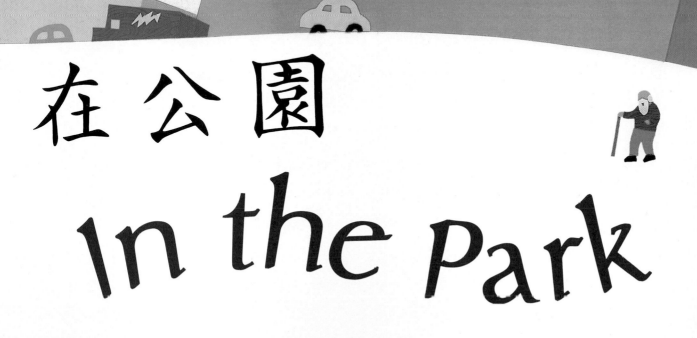

在公園
In the Park

written and illustrated by Huy Voun Lee

Henry Holt and Company • New York

Spring has brought sunshine, green leaves, and gentle breezes. Xiao Ming runs outside.

"Look, Mom, everyone is outside
having fun. Let's go to the park!"
"All right," his mother says.
"We can learn some new Chinese
characters there."

土 "I love spring," Xiao Ming says.

"I do too," says his mother. "Spring is a new beginning. Trees turn green and everything is bright again. The earth becomes rich and soft, and grass and flowers begin to grow." She picks up a stick and draws the character for *earth*.

"It looks like a plant growing," Xiao Ming says.

早 "In the spring," Xiao Ming's mother says, "plants grow because the sun wakes up early and makes the days warmer. In the springtime, people wake up early too. They want to enjoy the sunny days.

"I'll show you how to draw the character for *early*. See, it looks like the sun has come out to give light to the plants."

蟲 "Plants make good homes for *insects*!" says Xiao Ming. "I know how to draw that character. It looks like three bugs flying."

鳥 "Insects make good food for birds," says his mother. "In ancient times, people drew the character for *bird* a different way, but today, they draw it like this."

"I like the new way," says Xiao Ming. "Those four strokes look like feathers!"

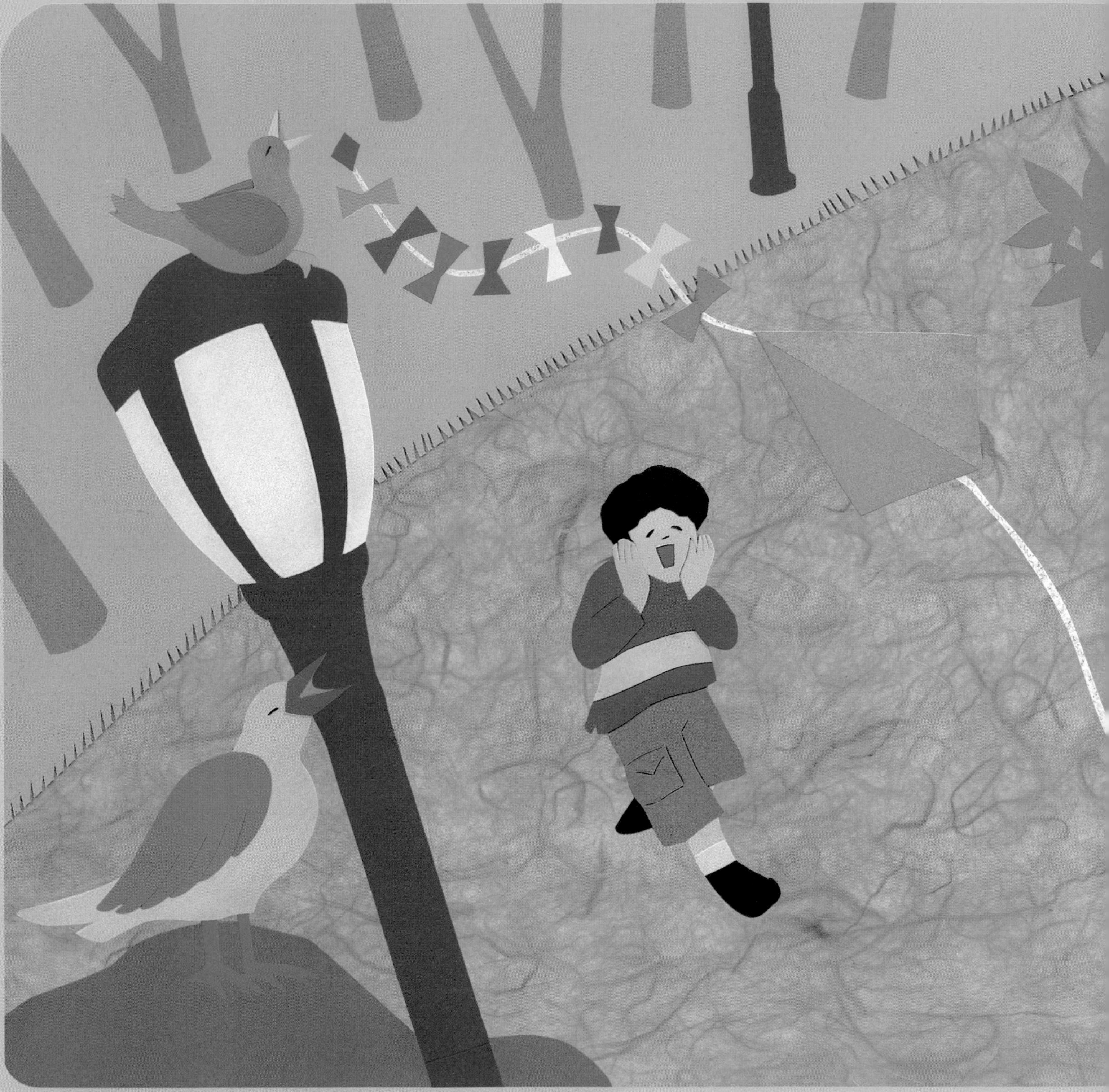

鳴 "Can you hear the birds chirping?" Xiao Ming's mother asks as they continue their walk.

Xiao Ming stops to listen.

"Birds have to open their mouths to sing," his mother says. "If you add the character for *mouth* to the character for *bird*, you have the character for *chirping*."

果 Xiao Ming practices drawing the new characters. Then he looks around the park and sees blossoms on the fruit trees.

"The old character for *fruit tree* had a tree with four fruits growing on top," his mother says. "But now the easiest way to remember how to draw it is to draw the character for *tree* 木 under the character for *field* 田."

"Like a field where fruit trees grow?" asks Xiao Ming.

"That's right," his mother says.

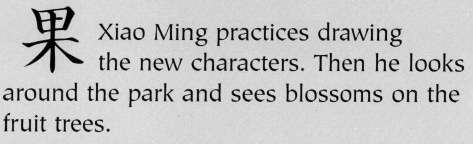

巢 "Look!" Xiao Ming is excited. He shows
his mother a nest in the tree. His mother
shows him how to draw the character for *nest*.
"Draw the character for *fruit tree*," she tells him.
"Then draw three bent lines over it."

"Those lines look like twigs," says Xiao Ming.
"That character is easy to remember."

川 Xiao Ming and his mother walk until they come to a stream.

"What does this look like to you?" she asks Xiao Ming as she stops to draw.

"It looks like water flowing," Xiao Ming says. "It must be the character for *stream*."

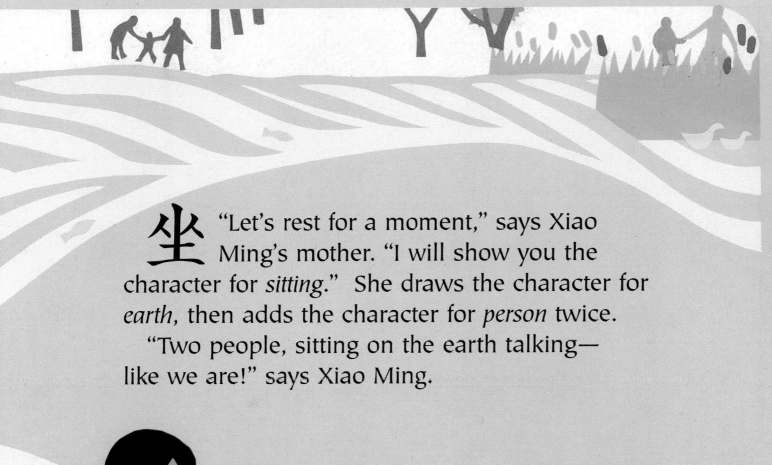

坐 "Let's rest for a moment," says Xiao Ming's mother. "I will show you the character for *sitting*." She draws the character for *earth*, then adds the character for *person* twice.

"Two people, sitting on the earth talking— like we are!" says Xiao Ming.

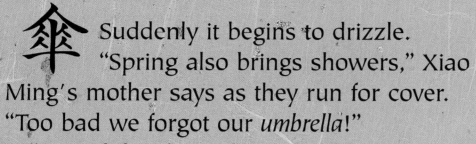 Suddenly it begins to drizzle.
"Spring also brings showers," Xiao Ming's mother says as they run for cover. "Too bad we forgot our *umbrella*!"

"But I didn't forget how to draw it," says Xiao Ming. "See, it looks like people sharing one big roof. Like a family."

"Like us," says his mother. "Like us in the park on a warm day in spring."

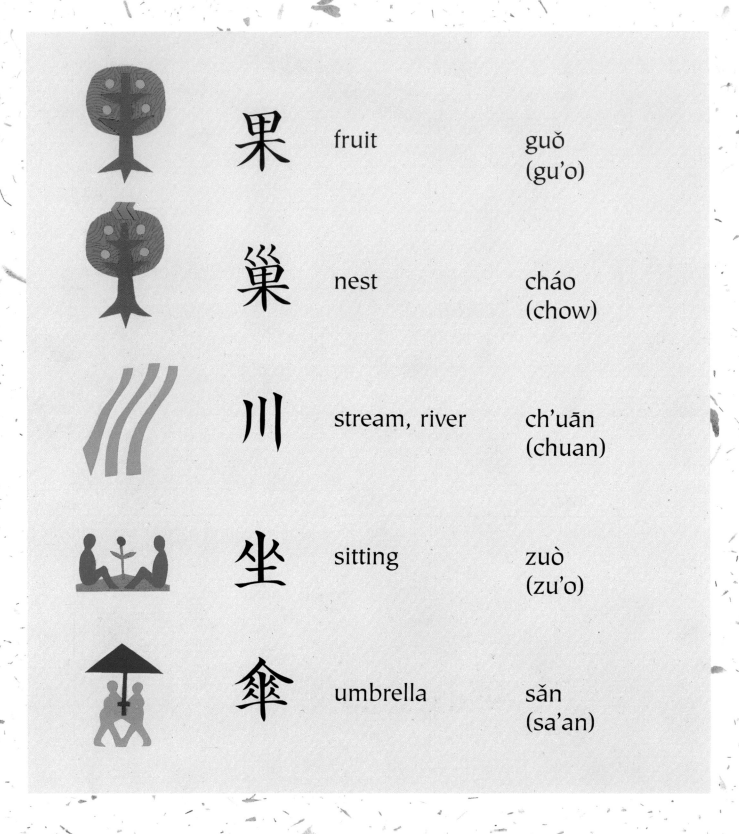

果   fruit   guǒ
(gu'o)

巢   nest   cháo
(chow)

川   stream, river   ch'uān
(chuan)

坐   sitting   zuò
(zu'o)

傘   umbrella   sǎn
(sa'an)